Amish Park

Amish Park

A novel
by
Thomas Nye

Dove
Publishers

Amish Park
Published by Dove Christian Publishers
P.O. Box 611
Bladensburg, MD 20710-0611
www.dovechristianpublishers.com

Cover photo by Robyn Rasmussen
Cover Design by Raenita Wiggins

Library of Congress Control Number: 2017951981

ISBN: 978-0-9986690-1-4

Printed in the United States of America

To my wife, Shari.
Thank you for standing by my side while I learn what it means to be a husband, father, and grandfather.

Getting There

"This is ridiculous, our family spending a week at Amish Park!" Pete shouted.

"Why do you have to yell everything?" his wife asked. She stood in front of a large mirror surrounded by lights, putting on eyeliner. Pete stopped packing his suitcase and looked at Lisa. She had straightened her long black hair; her skin was dark from the tanning beds she often visited. Her wrists, neck, and ears sparkled with jewelry. For a split second, his mind flashed back to how she looked during high school. Back then, Lisa, a softball pitcher, always wore her hair in a ponytail and never wore makeup. She didn't seem to be the same person anymore.

"I'm not yelling!" he shouted. "And why don't you ever look at me when we are having a conversation?"

"We don't have conversations; we fight," Lisa said, without looking away from her mirror.

"I'm trying to have a conversation with you right now!"

"Maybe when you stop yelling, I will look at you," she answered very quietly. Pete knew she did it to prove a point. Whenever they argued, he raised his voice, and Lisa would mutter something quietly. He sat on the edge of the bed and ran his fingers through his hair and inhaled deeply several times as his therapist had instructed.

Pete looked at Lisa and tried to speak without yelling. "Listen, marriage counseling failed, and our divorce papers are filed. Why are we taking our daughters on a family vacation?"

Lisa stopped putting on makeup for a moment and looked at her husband with disgust, the only expression he ever saw on her face. Lisa looked back into the mirror and said in her quiet, annoying way. "Just put up with your family for one more week. When we get back home, you can tell our daughters about the divorce. Then you can go to your high-powered executive office and bury yourself in your work that you love so much. We will leave you alone."

"Oh, so this is all my fault!" he yelled.

"Dad, please pack your suitcase; we need to get going." The sweet voice of his youngest daughter contrasted his wife's bitter tone and his angry shouts. Pete looked at Natalie, who was standing at the bedroom doorway, and wondered if she heard what they had been talking about.

Pete walked toward Natalie. "Are you all packed and ready?" he asked.

She nodded. "Dad, Carrie is just lying on her bed looking at her phone. Can you make her get ready?" Natalie looked at her dad with pleading eyes.

Pete followed his younger daughter through their large suburban Chicago home, toward his older daughter's room. He watched Natalie's ten-year-old form as they went. He felt sad that his little girl was so excited about this trip and couldn't get her family going. Taking hold of her small shoulders, he stopped her for a moment.

"Natalie, I'm really proud of you for planning this family vacation all by yourself."

She looked into his eyes and nodded.

Her sweet face made Pete smile, as always. "I'll get Carrie out the door. Did you print off the directions to this Amish Park?"

"Yes, Dad. Can we please get going?"

Pete stepped into his oldest daughter's room. Sixteen-year-old Carrie was lying on her bed, earbuds in, listening to music and tapping on her phone screen. Pete flicked her bedroom light on and off to get her attention. "We are leaving here in fifteen minutes. If you aren't packed, I will carry you out the door and whatever you have in that suitcase."

"Dad, there's nothing in my suitcase, yet."

"Fine, I'll take it empty. We are going to leave in fifteen minutes!"

"Stop yelling at me." Carrie looked at him. She had his blue eyes and light-brown hair, but the same disgusted look on her face her mother always had. He flashed five fingers three times to emphasize his point and walked out.

An hour later, they were in Pete's Escalade, gliding over rolling hills on the interstate. Everyone in the vehicle was scowling except little Natalie, whose face was beaming.

"Natalie, can you give me the paperwork from Amish Park? I want to look it over," Pete asked.

Natalie pulled an envelope from her handbag and passed it to her dad. He looked at a self-addressed envelope with Natalie's handwriting on it. "They sent you information in an envelope you sent them? What kind of place is this?"

"Don't yell," Lisa scolded.

"I'm just saying, I took the time to look at the website; couldn't you have looked at the letter they sent us?" he asked his wife.

"I thought you looked at it." She flashed a look of disgust. Pete pulled out a handwritten letter from the envelope. He tried to read it while driving, but Lisa snatched it from his hand. "I'll read; you drive."

> *Dear Natalie,*
> *Greetings in the blessed name of our Lord Jesus Christ. "All things work together for good to them that love God."*

We would be very pleased to have you and your family come and stay on our farm for a week. June 15th through 20th would be as good a week as any, even though we should be done planting corn by then. Don't worry, though; there will be plenty of work still to be done. We may be making hay or butchering early chickens while you are here. There is always gardening to be done and other odd jobs. Some folks have a hard time finding our place, so we are sending a map and directions.

We look forward to meeting your family and spending some time together.

In Christ's name, Mrs. Jonas Yoder

Lisa held out a hand-drawn map. "Natalie, how did you find out about this place?"

"My friend Elaine and her family went to Amish Park last summer. She said that it was the best time their family ever had!" Natalie's face glowed in Pete's rearview mirror.

Lisa whispered to Pete. "Didn't you say you looked at this place on the Internet?"

"Yes, I spent about an hour looking at the website. It's a tourist trap in Indiana that set up a farm in the middle of an Amish community. They try to make everything as close to the Amish way of living as possible for their guests. Guests stay in a farmhouse, dress like the Amish, and they give hayrides and serve family-style meals. It actually looked fun, but it didn't say anything about helping with farm work on the website."

"Oh great, Dad," Carrie moaned from her seat. "You didn't tell me I was going to have to dress Amish! Why did I have to pack all of my clothes if we are going to a place like that?"

"Carrie, don't be silly," Pete said. "We aren't going to spend all day on the farm. There will be some other attractions nearby, I'm sure." He looked in his rearview mirror at his oldest daughter. She didn't return his stare but made a disgusted face for his benefit.

Lisa whispered to her husband, "Didn't you get a confirmation number from this website? They should have sent us a brochure or something."

"Don't worry; I checked the availability online. I gave them my credit card numbers, and everything went through. Natalie said she had a letter from Amish Park, so I assumed it was a packet of information and directions."

Lisa laughed, and Pete glanced at her to see if she was making fun of him. She held up the hand-drawn map again and said, "Well, I guess they went to extremes to be as authentic as possible."

"Natalie, how did it happen that you sent them a self-addressed envelope?" Pete asked. "That's the part I don't understand." He looked at his little girl in the rearview mirror. Her eyes were sparkling.

"Before you signed us up for a week, I looked over the website for a while. They had a place on the web page asking for information about our family so they would know us better; to help them decide which house family to assign us to stay with. I couldn't figure out how to download it, so I sent a letter telling them about us, and they sent back this." She pointed at the letter her mother held.

Pete looked at his wife and whispered, "I remember her asking me for help; I told her to figure it out herself."

Lisa gave her husband another disgusted look.

Pete defended himself. "It's good for her to learn how to navigate the Internet; I was busy!"

"Is there any chance that while we are on this Amish farm, you will be able to make it a whole week without yelling?" Lisa asked in her annoying quiet voice.

"Do you think you can go a week without pouring over the details about your patients? These Amish folks don't want to hear sad stories about sick children. Our family needs a week off from all of that as well."

"I'll make a deal with you," Lisa said. "If you promise to keep your temper under control, I'll do my best not to bring up my patients or the Children's Hospital."

"It's a deal," Pete said.

He turned his Escalade off the interstate. In a short time, a buggy came into view. They looked closely as the buggy passed by and could see an Amish family riding along in old-fashioned clothes.

"Are those the costumes we have to wear?" Carrie asked.

"It'll be fun," Lisa said. "Before we go out for the evening we will shower, put our makeup on and forget about all that."

"C'mon you guys," Natalie begged. "Let's try to have fun as a family this last time."

Pete and Lisa met eyes nervously. Carrie didn't flinch; either she knew her parents were thinking about a divorce, or she didn't care.

Pete drove his Escalade through a touristy area with large hotels and restaurants. Huge billboards touted slogans about Amish food. Pictures of Amish buggies were on every sign. Pete entered the Yoders' address in his GPS while Lisa fumbled with the hand-drawn map.

"There should be some signs around here about Amish Park," Pete said. "Natalie, you watch for a billboard, and I will keep an eye on my GPS."

The GPS kept them heading straight on, right through town and out the other side. The road narrowed as they headed farther out into the boondocks. They all stared out the windows at white Amish farmhouses with matching barns and beautiful gardens full of flowers and growing vegetables.

"Turn right here," Lisa said.

"Turn left on G-38," The GPS voice spoke at the same instant.

Pete swung his SUV to the right and pulled over. "Now, which is it? Our GPS says turn left, and you said turn right."

"Don't yell. I meant to say turn left, right here."

Pete whipped his Escalade into a driveway of an Amish farm

to turn around. Little girls in Amish dresses were working in a garden; they waved in a friendly way. A young boy with a straw hat was riding a pony in a nearby field, and he waved as well. Pete's family stared at them as if they were watching a science fiction movie. Pete backed his Escalade onto the road, threw the gear shift into drive, punched the accelerator, and they roared on down the blacktop road. They wound around curves for a few miles, watching Amish farms pass by. There were horses pulling buggies, cows grazing in fields and more barns than they had ever seen.

Suddenly, the GPS said, "Your destination in on the right."

Pete stopped and looked at a dirt drive which was heading up a hill. "This can't be the place!"

"Oh yes, it can." Lisa laughed and pointed at a mailbox marked with the same address and *Jonas Yoder* handwritten above. "It says here to 'take the dirt drive up over the hill. Where the drive splits, take the one that veers to the left. That's our lane. Go on through those trees, and you'll see our house.'"

Pete drove uphill and turned left as instructed. They passed through a row of trees, and a spectacular view appeared. A perfectly manicured Amish farm stood before them, lit up by the golden rays of a sunset. White barns and outbuildings surrounded two houses, one huge and one tiny, situated in a valley with white fences bordering everything. Brightly colored Amish dresses flapped on a clothesline, indicating a gentle breeze was blowing. Black-and-white Holstein cows grazed peacefully as the Escalade drove past. Massive work horses stood in harness near the house. A black and purple quilt hung over a porch railing and beyond that was the biggest garden they had ever seen.

Pete climbed down stiffly from his SUV as an elderly Amish man strolled out to meet them. The old man was difficult to see because of a red setting sun behind him. The Heller family squinted into the light as the older man reached out his hand to shake Pete's and spoke. "Hello, I'm Jonas Yoder."

"I'm Peter Heller; people just call me Pete. Pleased to meet you. This is my wife, Lisa, and our daughters, Carrie and Natalie."

The elderly man smiled at them all; then he turned his attention to the littlest. "Natalie, thank you for telling us about your family. I hope this week turns out to be good for all of us."

Natalie reached up and shook the older man's hand, her face beaming. In only a few moments, a group of Amish people gathered around in a large circle, all looking at the Heller family as if they were the first non-Amish people they had ever seen.

An older woman stepped forward. "We were beginning to wonder if you were still coming. Nice to meet you in person, Natalie. Your letter was very nice, and we hoped and prayed that your family would all come and spend time with us on the farm. It's getting late. 'Early to bed and early to rise'… as the saying goes, 'makes a man healthy, wealthy, and wise.' I'm Jonas' wife, Mattie. Come inside, and we'll show you where you will sleep."

Carrie gave her dad another grouchy look as they followed a large group of Amish people into an immaculately clean home. Gas lanterns swayed as they walked past, causing shadows to swirl. Mattie spoke in Dutch to a middle-sized girl. The girl spoke English with a thick accent. "You girls will sleep with us sisters. Bring your things upstairs with me."

She headed through a stairway door and up the stairs, and Natalie quickly followed. Carrie stood still, looking at her dad as if hoping he would tell her she didn't have to follow.

Pete pointed to the steps. "You'd better hurry, or you'll get lost in this big house." Everyone laughed.

Mattie spoke to Pete and Lisa. "This is our son's wife, Doreen; we call her Dory." They each shook hands with a very pleasant looking Amish woman, and she smiled at them. An Amish man with a dark black beard came walking in. "And this is our son Cephas; you two will have a lot in common," she said. Pete looked at the Amish man, who seemed to be about his age. He couldn't imagine having even one thing in common with this Cephas. They shook hands politely.

"We'll let you and your wife take our bedroom over there," Cephas said

"Oh, we couldn't do that," Lisa answered.

"No, it's fine, really," Dory explained. "We have another spare room upstairs. We usually give up our bedroom to guests. It is closer to the water closet."

"Water closet?" Lisa questioned.

"Bathroom," Dory explained.

The Farm

Morning light faintly glimmered on window shades. A 5:30 a.m. knock on the door woke Pete from a deep sleep. "Time to rise and shine," a voice called from beyond the door.

"Lisa, they are trying to wake us," Pete said.

She pulled the sheet up over her head.

Pete spoke louder. "Lisa, wake up."

She moaned and sat up on the edge of the bed. "I hope they don't plan on waking us up this early every day."

Pete and Lisa headed out into the kitchen and were greeted by the wonderful aroma of breakfast food sizzling on the stove.

Dory looked at Pete. "Most of the chores are done by now. If you want to get in on morning milking, you better get right out to the big barn." Lisa started to follow him, and Dory stopped her. "I could use your help in here if you don't mind."

"Oh, of course." Pete heard his wife answer and chuckled to himself as he hurried out toward the barn.

He walked past a group of Amish children and was surprised to see his daughters were helping feed baby calves with plastic bottles. He was stunned that his girls were laughing and having fun. Pete ventured into the belly of the large barn and found teenage girls singing hymns while they milked cows. Pete thought it was odd they were wearing dresses to do a job like that, and even more shocked to notice they were barefoot.

He listened to their hymns for a few moments. There were large sliding doors opened on either end of the barn, offering beautiful views of lush rolling hills lined with white fences, and farther away, Amish farms. A cow let out a deep bellow, which echoed off concrete feed bunks and made Pete jump. The girls noticed him. One spoke.

"Good morning; our dad is just beyond those doors, feeding hay."

Pete stepped outside. A small square bale fell out of the sky, causing him to jump again. The bale made a loud thump as it landed in a wooden bunk a few feet away. A man's laughter could be heard from above, and Pete leaned back out through the doorway. Cephas was looking down from the hayloft.

"Don't worry; I've thrown a lot of bales into that feed bunk over the years. I don't miss very often."

"Is there anything I can do to help?" Pete called.

"Pull the twine strings off those bales," Cephas answered.

Pete reached into one side of the bunk while cows stuck their heads in from the opposite side. He breathed in a sweet smell of hay and warm air that had no doubt been exhaled by a cow. He looked at a rubbery cow nose pushing into hay bales greedily, pulling off tufts to eat. The cows stared at Pete suspiciously, while he tried to yank off twine strings. He had only pulled off two strings before Cephas appeared beside him and quickly finished the other six bales.

"Let's go carry milk," Cephas said, as he headed back to the dairy barn.

Stainless steel cans about knee-high were waiting for them. Cephas lifted one and Pete hefted up the other and followed the Amish man into a nearby room with an enormous stainless steel tank. Cephas easily hoisted his container, dumping creamy-white milk into a large vat. Pete tried to raise his container high enough but struggled. Cephas reached out and helped, until milk began to pour out, lightening the load. Pete noticed how amazingly fresh it smelled.

"Let's bring some of this milk in with us for breakfast," Cephas said while filling a glass pitcher from a tap at the bottom of his milk-tank. The teenage Amish girls were still singing hymns as they pushed brooms across the floor where cows had been standing a short time ago. Pete and Cephas passed by their children and baby calves. Natalie and Carrie were helping load hay into small feed bunks and giggling at the tiny black-and-white cows.

Pete couldn't help wondering how long the others had been up working before he joined them. He followed his Amish guide through a set of cellar doors and down into a cool, immaculately clean basement. They washed up in a basin of water which sat on a counter. Before they were finished, the children had come down the steps, and one-by-one washed up in the same water. Pete was surprised his daughters imitated the Amish girls. However, he saw Carrie making an icky face as she did. They all dried off with the same small towel, which hung nearby.

Everyone took seats on long benches around a huge table. Cephas said to his children, "Put your hands down and let's pray." His children were all quietly sitting before he spoke, and Pete gathered that it was an expression. They all bowed, and nothing was said. Finally, Cephas said a faint, "Amen." His large family began to pass around bowls of eggs and fried potatoes.

On one side of the table, Natalie sat between two little Amish girls about her own age. Carrie and two teenage Amish girls were squeezed in beyond them. Pete tried to guess if either of the girls were her age but couldn't tell. Cephas sat at one end, and his oldest boy was next and a younger brother beside him. Pete and Lisa sat next to each other, and a highchair with a little boy wearing cloth suspenders sat between Lisa and Dory.

"Reach and help yourselves," Cephas said. As they passed food around Cephas introduced his family. "Our oldest is James," he pointed across the table with his fork. "Then comes our oldest daughter, Ada."

"I'm the same age as Carrie," Ada said with a smile.

"Then comes Edna," Cephas continued his introductions. "Stephen follows Edna, and then Ida is next."

"I'm the same age as Natalie," Ida chimed in.

"I'm almost as old as Natalie," the next little girl said.

"That's Orpha," Cephas added, "and then our baby is Toby."

"I don't think I can remember all of those names," Pete said.

"The girls' names are easy," Natalie told her dad. "Just think of the order of vowels, A, E, I, and O. Ada, Edna, Ida, and Orpha." The little girls on either side of Natalie both nodded and smiled at her. After that, everyone ate in awkward silence, until Natalie asked a question.

"Are we going to get to wear Amish clothes?" Lisa and Carrie laughed nervously, embarrassed at Natalie's boldness. Dory looked at her guests to see if they might be willing to wear Amish clothes. Natalie piped up again. "We all thought that it would be really fun to dress up in your clothes."

Carrie made a face of a person in shock.

"We could start sewing dresses for your mother and older sister after breakfast," Dory answered with a friendly voice. "I believe we already have extra dresses in your size, Natalie."

Natalie smiled with anticipation. Everything on the table was delicious, especially the fresh milk, which had cream floating around on its surface.

After the meal, Cephas explained, "We usually bow our heads after we eat, to thank God for what we have just received." Everyone bowed in silence for a few moments.

In the following bustle of activity, Carrie snuck close to her dad and whispered, "My phone is almost out of power."

"Plug it in," Pete answered with what seemed a simple and obvious solution.

"They don't seem to have electricity anywhere in this house."

"Oh, that's a problem." Pete looked at his phone and realized it would be dead soon, also. He asked out loud, "Is there a place we can plug in our phones? They are about ready to die."

"Did you need to call someone?" Cephas inquired.

"I guess not," Pete answered and saw Carrie's eyes get wide. He quickly added, "We may need to make a call or two before the week is over."

"We have a phone booth less than a mile away if it turns out you need to make a call," Cephas said.

Pete tried to think of how he could explain that he used his phone for a lot more than calling people.

Lisa smiled at her husband and commented, "That will be enough phone calls for our family this week."

Dory sent her husband to gather some clothes for Pete. While they waited, Carrie pulled her dad aside, whispering angry words into his ear. "They shut off their lanterns at 9:00 last night. I couldn't get to sleep for three hours, but at least I had my phone. Now, what will I do without my phone or Internet?"

"We'll try to get them charged when we go to town tonight," Pete whispered. His daughter almost gave him a smile but stopped short of it. Pete turned to walk away and bumped into Natalie. "I didn't know you were standing right beside me," Pete whispered.

"Dad, will you and Carrie please try to have fun here?" Natalie said, softly.

Pete nodded and looked at Carrie and raised his eyebrows. Carrie rolled her eyes in response.

Cephas came into the kitchen and handed his guest a pile of clothing. Pete headed into his bedroom to change. He struggled to figure out how to put on pants with a button-up flap. His wife had to help him get his suspenders in place. When Pete came out wearing Amish clothes, everyone smiled at him. Cephas tossed Pete a straw hat. "You'll need something to keep the sun off while we are working outside."

Sewing lessons were underway for Lisa and Carrie, as Pete

followed Cephas back outdoors for more farm work. Old Jonas joined Cephas and the boys as they headed out toward the big barn.

"Where do you live Jonas?" Pete ventured to ask.

"We live in the Grandpa House over there," Jonas pointed to a smaller white home next to Cephas' larger one.

"Grandpa House?" Pete questioned.

"Amish people don't send their elderly relatives to retirement homes; they let us live in Grandpa Houses on the farm."

Pete nodded that he understood and followed the group of men into the dark insides of a smaller barn which stood near the dairy barn. When his eyes adjusted, he realized he was looking at the hindquarters of draft horses. A long line of light-brown horses with blond tails stood tied in a row, facing in toward the center wall. They towered over the men, who were speaking quietly in Dutch. Pete concluded that Cephas and Jonas were discussing what work should be done, and what horses should be used to do it. One of Cephas' boys stood near Pete.

"This is Lady." The boy pointed at the first massive horse. "That is Manny, her teammate. Then next is Rocky, Jim, Bill, and Bob. Those down beyond them are just colts. We started breaking them this spring, and they are doing good."

"They don't look like colts," Pete said.

"They're real big colts," the boy answered with a smile. "We have several more mares out on pasture with new colts."

The men began dragging over horse harnesses, and Pete watched as four horses were made ready for work. He was stunned at how fearlessly they handled the enormous creatures. Even the young, barefoot boy slipped in between sets of thick-legged horses, helping to snap everything in place. They led their huge horses down a walkway. Each clip-clop of their massive hooves seemed to shake the ground and echo through the building. Pete couldn't believe his eyes as he watched them hitch two of the golden horses to a steel-wheeled contraption. Their thick round bodies seemed to ripple with muscle, and they raised their arched necks and snorted. He was even more surprised when the twelve-year-old boy was sent off, driving the magnificent beasts.

"Stephen will go rake hay with Rocky and Jim." Jonas explained, "James can haul some manure with Bill and Bob; we will use Lady and Manny on a stone-boat to make fence."

When the oldest boy, James, had his horses hitched to the manure spreader, Cephas and Pete helped the teenage boy fork a straw and manure mix which had been behind the long line of draft horses. The big blond team of horses stood quietly while the three of them filled the wagon box with rich-smelling cargo. Jonas disappeared while they did the heavy work.

After both boys were sent off to the fields driving huge horses, the older men hitched another set of big horses to a flat sled. They loaded the sled with tools and supplies for making a fence. Cephas and Jonas stepped on and motioned for their guest to join them. Pete cautiously stepped in beside them. Jonas shook his driving lines and clucked, sending both horses off with a jerk. Pete instinctively grabbed hold of something to keep from falling, and then realized he was almost hugging Cephas. The two men looked at each other awkwardly. Pete had a suspicious feeling Cephas didn't like him, and that he would rather not have a strange family in his home.

Once they were moving forward, it wasn't difficult to balance and stay upright. Pete smiled while watching the beautiful horses pulling them over a lush green pasture. They stopped under a shade tree and set to work on a fence which was already half erected. Birds sat on branches and sang above them. A gentle breeze blew the scent of hay which Stephen and his horses were raking and the odor of manure that James and his horses were spreading.

Pete watched his Amish counterparts set posts in holes which had been created earlier. They worked without words, and Pete picked up on how they went about their business, and he soon joined in. He found it fun to kick dirt in around posts and tamp it down with a wooden pole made for that purpose. While they were working, a little pony came trotting near, pulling a tiny cart. Three little Amish girls were riding on the seat. As they got closer, Pete realized one of them was his daughter, Natalie.

"We brought out some tea for you to drink," one of the girls called.

They filled up a glass and gave it to Pete. He took his time sipping a wonderfully sweet mint tea until he realized they were waiting for him to finish so they could pass the same glass to Jonas and Cephas.

"Isn't this fun?" Natalie asked.

The others looked at Pete to see what his answer would be. "Oh, yeah; it sure is," he answered, and Jonas smiled. Pete watched his daughter and the other little Amish girls head off toward Stephen and the hayfield and assumed they were going to share a drink of tea with him. He turned around and realized Jonas and Cephas were already back to work.

Making fence wasn't extremely hard work; however, after several hours of it, Pete felt he was about ready to pass out if he didn't sit down soon. A bell rang in the distance.

"Mealtime," Jonas announced.

They stopped what they were doing and stepped onto their stone-boat and watched huge horses pulling them toward home.

"Why don't we let Pete try driving Manny and Lady?" Jonas said to his son. Cephas passed the lines to his guest.

"I don't have any idea how to drive a team of horses," Pete explained, while he took the lines.

"Keep both lines even and not too tight, but not too loose," Jonas said. He reached over and showed Pete what he meant. "If you want to turn right put a little more tension on this right line. Go ahead give it a try."

Pete gently took in some of the right line, and both horses immediately began moving right, out into the open pasture.

"Now, pull on the left line to turn them back," Jonas explained.

Power coursed through the lines and through chains which attached the horses to the sled. Instantly, Pete felt a surge of adrenaline in his heart, and a smile came to his face. He was disappointed when they reached the barn and tied the horses. He hoped he would get a chance to try driving horses again.

After they had done the basement wash-up routine, they all gathered around Dory's table for another huge meal. Lisa and Carrie were wearing crisp new Amish dresses with white aprons. Pete looked at his wife in unbelief. She looked so young with her hair in a bun under a scarf, and no makeup on. She returned his gaze as if not sure what he was thinking. Carrie didn't even raise her eyes. It wasn't clear if she was humiliated or mad. Natalie sat between her little Amish friends, and they whispered to each other and smiled throughout the noon meal. When bowls of food were passed around the second time, only the Amish family took more.

"Sorry, we aren't used to eating so much good food," Lisa explained.

The afternoon passed much like the morning. James hauled more manure, Stephen raked hay, and Cephas, Jonas and their guest "made fence." Pete could see Amish women near the house and surmised that Dory had found a way to get Lisa and Carrie to work in her garden. He chuckled to himself at the thought of the two of them with dirty hands.

While the Amish men strung up fence wires, Jonas took the time to explain what they were doing. "This is a fence stretcher; we call it a *come-a-long*. We put a brace between end-posts. See how that brace angles down from the top of our corner post to near the ground on the next post. That lets us pull wires tight; our corner-post is braced up and doesn't start to lean inward."

"I see. For years, I've driven past fences and never took the time to notice how they were made."

"What do you do for work?" Jonas questioned.

"I'm a CEO of a software company. We make computer programs designed to help small businesses manage finances and keep in touch with tax issues. There is a ton of pressure on me to keep the company afloat, and my wife doesn't seem to understand that."

"You said you're a CEO?"

"Chief executive officer. It's code for, 'I get paid the most to make sure everyone else does all the work,'" Pete said and laughed.

Cephas gave him a scowl, and Jonas' face worked at a grin. The older man said, "Maybe you could give us some ideas about how to manage our small business?"

"From what I've seen so far, you have a great business plan going here," Pete said, and he and Jonas exchanged a friendly look.

Natalie and her little Amish friends came out bouncing on a cart behind their little pony, bringing more sweet tea. One of the girls announced, "Mom wants you men to quit early. We are going to Marcus's for supper."

Natalie pointed to a white Amish farm which sat on top of a hill in the distance. "That is Jonas' oldest son's place. They invited us to come for a meal." She seemed as excited as could be. Pete opened his mouth to decline their offer. His eyes met Natalie's, and he remembered her sweet pleading words: "*Try to have fun here.*"

"Oh, that sounds fun," Pete said, without enthusiasm. He was tired and sore from working all day in the hot sun and had been hoping for a shower, a quick meal, and a relaxing movie.

3

Supper Out

Pete and Lisa had a few moments to talk in the bedroom before they left for "supper out." She scolded him. "I thought you told me we could clean up in the evenings and do our own thing."

"I thought we would," Pete whispered so the Amish people wouldn't hear him. "I'll talk to Jonas and try to explain that we want a little family time for ourselves."

Lisa had to stare at his mouth to catch what he was saying. "Well, at least you are whispering here and not yelling," she said quietly.

"At least you are looking at me when I talk," he quipped, and they both laughed quietly.

"Please," Lisa begged, "don't have one of your yelling fits while we are here on the farm."

Pete looked at his wife and opened his mouth to yell.

Lisa quickly put a finger to her mouth, like a mother hushing a child. "Please, for Natalie's sake."

Pete raised both hands in frustration.

***

Cephas' family hurried out the door as though excited about their evening plans. Pete and his family, dressed in Amish clothes, headed for their Escalade. Jonas was standing near a hitching rack with Lady and Manny harnessed and hitched to a hay wagon. He called over. "No reason to use up your gasoline; ride along with us."

"I don't want to make more work for your horses. We will follow your family over."

"Lady and Manny took the afternoon off; they won't even notice a few extra people. We are only going a short way," Jonas protested.

Pete looked at his family, and they didn't even glance at him. As if they knew there wasn't any use arguing with an elderly Amish man, they quietly walked over and climbed aboard.

It was a lovely evening and almost impossible not to enjoy sitting on hay bales and riding behind a team of horses. They headed down a shady dirt road along the ridge of the hill between Jonas' farm and his son Marcus' place. Rich green fields sprawled out in every direction as far as the eye could see. Black and white dairy cows grazed peacefully. Pete looked at the new fence he had helped make. Beautiful lines marked out where Stephen had turned over rows of hay during the afternoon, and they couldn't help taking in the wonderful fresh aroma. Pete felt almost renewed by the time they arrived at the neighbor's place for supper and assumed his family did as well.

A large group of Amish girls, in a variety of brightly colored plain dresses, stood in a circle around them when they pulled into the drive. It wasn't clear what type of gathering it was until Jonas explained.

"Our son, Marcus, has only daughters, but he has ten of them." He smiled as though quite pleased about it.

The Amish girls looked like stair steps, all the way down to toddlers who were as cute as could be in their teeny Amish dresses and aprons. The whole group of girls gathered around Carrie and Natalie and began jabbering as though they were long lost friends. In only a few minutes, they had whisked a tiny baby into Carrie's arms, and her face lit up.

With Cephas' four daughters, Marcus's ten, plus Pete's daughters and all their wives, the house was filled with the music of female voices. Pete thought the sound reminded him of birds in the spring. Everything hushed to a perfect silence when Marcus said, "Put your hands down, let's pray."

A few minutes passed by. Marcus coughed, and the music of female voices resumed in full force. All three families sat around two large tables that held mountains of chicken and mashed potatoes. Pete didn't think he could eat again for a week after they finally stopped passing food around. The whole mass of women had everything cleared and spotless faster than one of the girls could've said, "Jack Robinson." All at once, everyone headed outside as if on cue. Pete's family followed.

Cool evening air added to an already almost surreal experience. Pete had a fleeting thought that this moment on an Amish farm was about as close to heaven as anything he had experienced. Marcus's house and barns were just as white as Cephas'. His pastures and fields were equally green. His wife's garden was even bigger than Dory's, and as they walked past it, Pete searched for one weed and couldn't find it.

The mass of girls gathered under a huge oak tree which sat on the edge of a hill. They were such a crowd that Pete couldn't see what the excitement was until Jonas told him. "There's a swing on the hillside that they love to ride."

"How do you tell all of your daughters apart?" Lisa asked.

Marcus seemed happy to explain. "My wife has a good plan; each daughter wears a certain color. We can tell which of our girls is which even when they are way out in the field, just by her dress color."

"They don't have any choice about what color dress they wear?" Lisa questioned.

"When they make a church dress, they can choose, but for around our home place, they have a color."

The adults moved a little closer so they could watch as the girls rode a swing way out over a hill. Everything was situated perfectly, with a tree limb hanging out above a steep drop-off.

"You have to try this, Mom," Natalie exclaimed. "It's so fun; you won't believe it!"

Everyone looked at Lisa, and she shook her head.

"Pete, you give your wife a push on that swing," Jonas ordered with a smile.

Everyone was watching, and Pete didn't feel he could refuse. Lisa hesitated to take a seat.

"Hurry up, everyone is watching," Pete whispered.

Lisa's soft shoulders were warm as he reached out to push her. He wondered how long it had been since he had even touched his wife. Lisa laughed in a girlish giggle as the swing swooped out over the field.

"Oh, this tickles my stomach!" she called. After a few pushes, she begged her husband. "Please stop me!"

As Lisa came floating back, Pete reached around her to stop the motion, almost with a hug. Lisa looked into his eyes, laughing, and quickly looked away. She looked around at everyone else and said with a smile. "Natalie was right; it was fun." Everyone laughed.

All the men walked toward a big white barn. A lone horse was trotting in circles, harnessed to a contraption which looked like a merry-go-round.

"What's this horse doing?" Pete dared to ask.

"Marcus built a horse-powered ice cream maker." Jonas' eyes twinkled as he answered.

"What, that horse is making ice cream?"

"Yes, exactly," Marcus laughed. "Homemade ice cream is fun to crank by the half-gallon, but when we have company over, we need several gallons, so we let one of our buggy horses do the cranking."

"Whoa, that's wild," Pete called out, and the horse stopped.

Marcus spoke to his horse. "Giddyap," and it stepped into

a trot again.

"My horse took your 'whoa' as an order," Marcus whispered and laughed.

The men stood and visited about hay making while watching the horse trotting in circles.

"We will be ready to bale hay as soon as the sun gets high enough tomorrow," Cephas said.

Marcus took off his straw hat, scratched his head, and put his hat back on. "We will all be there to help as soon as chores and breakfast are done," he answered.

"Could you bring over your baler? We have so many hands to help, we might as well have both balers running," Cephas asked.

Pete took off his straw hat and scratched his head. He was feeling sore from making the fence and was hoping tomorrow would not be a work day. Marcus snuck in to check on his ice cream, ducking as the horse walked past, attached to a bar which cranked the machine.

"Ice cream is ready!" Marcus called. He said "whoa" to his horse, and it stood still. He unsnapped and led the horse to a nearby stall while Cephas took the ice cream over to a large picnic table.

Jonas filled bowls with ice cream while the women brought out huge bowls of chopped homegrown strawberries. Everyone added strawberries to their bowls. Pete shut his eyes in pleasure with each bite.

"This is the creamiest ice cream I've ever had, and I've never tasted such sweet strawberries in my life!" Pete said.

"My daughters picked the strawberries this morning, and I did sprinkle some sugar on them as I chopped them up," Marcus' wife admitted.

Pete nodded but couldn't stop eating long enough to make a comment. Old Jonas noticed when Pete scraped his bowl clean.

"Let me dip you out another bowl of ice cream," Jonas said with a smile.

Pete thought he should turn him down. Before he could refuse, Jonas took his bowl and filled it with ice cream and passed it back. Marcus' wife pushed the bowl of strawberries in his direction. She smiled and nodded encouragement to Pete, prompting him to douse his ice cream with more of her amazing strawberry topping.

A brilliant, glowing sunset filled the sky as the visiting families climbed aboard their hay wagon and said good-byes. Marcus, his wife, and ten daughters all stood in a large clump and waved as the horses pulled out of the lane and headed toward the setting sun.

"We'll be over to help make hay tomorrow," Marcus called with his hands cupped to his mouth to direct his voice.

Hay Day

Pete heard a knock at the bedroom door. Dory's voice called from beyond, "Time to rise and shine; it's a hay day!"

Pete shook his wife's shoulder and said, "Lisa, they are trying to wake us up."

"We just laid down, didn't we?" Lisa said and moaned.

"It seems like it, but I heard a knock on our door, and they are already talking about us helping make hay," Pete said.

"You will be making hay, us women will probably stay inside," Lisa replied smugly.

Pete took in a breath of farm-fresh air when he walked down the porch steps. A rooster crowed in the distance, and a cow bellowed. White clouds, only a few feet above the ground, hung in the valley between Marcus' farm and Cephas' place. The heavenly, white fog matched Marcus' house and barns. Beautiful hay aromas filled the air riding on a soft morning breeze. Pete walked past a group of little Amish girls feeding calves.

"Where is Carrie?" Pete asked Natalie.

"She is inside learning how to milk a cow," Natalie answered matter-of-factly.

Pete hurried inside, curious about how that would go. He found Carrie sitting on a tiny wooden chair next to a cow. She looked as Amish as the other girls, with her long dress and white apron. Before Pete could say anything, he heard Cephas' voice.

"Let's see if you can catch onto milking a cow as quickly as your daughter."

Pete spent the next ten minutes struggling to hook a set of four silver vacuum tubes onto a huge black-and-white cow's udder. The cow began to grow tired of his clumsy attempts and finally kicked the unit out of his hand.

"Carrie, will you come show your dad how this is done?" Cephas said it as if he wanted to rub it in that his daughter was catching on more quickly than Pete.

Carrie stepped in beside the cow, and within a moment, she had connected all four silver tubes onto the large cow's udder. She met eyes with her dad and gave a look he couldn't quite place. He wasn't sure if she was taunting him or looking for his approval.

***

After breakfast, Cephas' family stood up, and Pete's family followed their lead. They all headed out to the horse barn, except for Dory and Lisa.

"We'll start working on lunch," Dory announced.

Jonas was already hitching a huge team of horses to a small steel-wheeled cart. He then drove the cart near a large machine shed as Cephas slid open the doors. They hooked the horse cart onto a flat rack which had a gas-powered engine mounted on it. Finally, a hay-baling implement was attached to the engine. Cephas fired up the engine, and Jonas headed off to bale hay. Cephas and his older children harnessed up two more teams of horses and hitched them to hayracks. Everyone, including the little children, climbed aboard one wagon or the other, and they rode out to the hayfield.

"My dad will let the bales drop on the ground," Cephas explained." We have so much help today it will be easier to keep the baler going, and we all can pick up bales and load wagons. Once we get a wagon full, some of us can go stack hay while others stay out here and pick up bales."

Everyone nodded that they understood or didn't know enough about what was said even to ask a question. Cephas spoke to his daughters in Dutch. His daughter, Ida, who was Natalie's age, climbed up on a hayrack and took hold of the driving lines.

"Natalie, come up here with me," Ida called.

The oldest sister, Ada, took the lines of the other hay wagon and said, "Carrie, you can ride along with me!"

Within moments, the teams of horses were following Jonas and his bailing machine. Cephas and his boys started picking up bales and tossing them to the girls on the wagons. Pete set off doing the same.

They hadn't fully loaded one wagon, when Pete noticed a hayrack full of Amish girls at the far end of the field, heading toward them. Marcus was following close behind with his horse-drawn baling contraption.

Soon, both ends of the field were alive with purring and clunking of gas-powered engines thumping out fresh green hay bales.

"Our wagon is full enough," Cephas announced. "Let's head to the barn and start putting hay up."

Cephas and his sons jumped onto the hayrack and motioned for Pete to get on. He struggled to climb aboard because hay bales were stacked high and close to the edge. Carrie and Ada were sitting on a platform of bales, driving the horses. Cephas reached down and offered a hand-up to his guest, but he looked frustrated, as though he didn't enjoy the whole 'Amish Park' thing.

From that point on the men were stuck inside the hot haymow, stacking bales. Every time they finished unloading one wagon a team of horses appeared, hauling another wagon full of hay to be put up. Pete didn't even try to keep up with the others. Even twelve-year-old Stephen moved bales faster than he could.

As tired as he was, Pete couldn't help taking pleasure in the wonderful, rich aroma of freshly baled hay. The moment Pete felt he couldn't take any more hay stacking, he saw Lisa standing at the doorway.

"Lunchtime," she called.

Both large families gathered around picnic tables heavy laden with food. Fresh fruits and vegetables were in big bowls. Slices of ham and cheese were on plates next to homemade bread all cut into thick pieces. They all bowed in silent prayer. Pete muttered a prayer in his own heart for the first time in years. *"Lord, please help me get my family off this farm, at least for a day."*

Everyone loaded up plates and found a place to sit. Some sat around the tables, some on the porch-swing. Jonas, Cephas, and Pete sat in chairs which had been brought out under a shade tree. A breeze blew through the branches overhead and passed across the men who sat in shady coolness. Pete's shirt was soaking wet with sweat, but it started to dry while he ate. Natalie and Carrie were difficult to pick out in the massive group of Amish girls sitting on hay bales and chattering like starlings. Jonas spoke up, his deep voice contrasting the girls twittering.

"Tomorrow we will come to your place, Marcus, and help you make hay."

"I had plans to take my family on a day trip tomorrow if that would be okay?" Pete said. Everyone got quiet, and Pete noticed his wife giving him a scowl.

"Dad, could I stay here and help make hay?" Carrie's voice sounded surprisingly sweet.

"I want to stay on the farm, too," Natalie said, with a huge smile on her face.

Everyone laughed, and Pete shrugged his shoulders. "Maybe we could take our trip tomorrow evening?"

"That is fine with us," Jonas said, "It's up to you and your family."

"This afternoon Lisa and I will help put up hay," Dory said. "I don't want her to miss out on all the fun!"

"Good idea," Pete said and laughed for the first time all day. "I don't want her to miss out on the fun either!"

Everyone laughed at Pete's words, except Lisa. Pete could see her whisper in his direction. "Thanks."

Lisa and Dory took the job of tossing bales off the wagon. Pete, Cephas and Stephen carried and stacked bales inside the barn. Lisa looked as if she was having fun and making a contest out of trying to keep up with Dory. Pete took his time and didn't even try to keep up with the boy.

"Why don't you try a little harder. It looks like you don't want to help," Lisa whispered when she was near Pete.

"I'm mad at that Cephas for charging us a big price and then making us work so hard."

"Sshh, do you want him to hear you?"

"I'm going to tell him what I think before we leave," Pete said and lifted his eyebrows to show he meant it.

"Please don't," Lisa pleaded. "We wanted to know what life on an Amish farm is like, and that is what we are getting."

"Yeah, and Cephas is getting our money and his work done," Pete growled.

Lisa put her finger to her lips and gave her husband the eye.

***

It was almost dark when Marcus, his wife, and daughters gathered their littlest girls and headed home to start their evening chores. The sun hung low in the west and rested on the horizon as Cephas' family quietly went about their evening chores, with their non-Amish visitors following along and helping with what they could. They all stopped on the large porch and sat down to watch the sun's last brilliant display of color before it sunk out of sight.

Crickets chirped out a merry song, while Dory cut open two large watermelons and passed around thick slices. She also brought out heaping containers of salted popcorn, and they helped themselves to all they could eat. Fireflies lit up as though carrying miniature lanterns. Natalie and the little Amish children ran around the yard trying to catch as many as they could. Stars blinked brightly above Cephas' farm, having no electric lights to compete with. When they finished slurping the last juices from their watermelon rinds, Dory said, "Let's sing a few songs."

"Yes, let's do!" Cephas' daughters chimed in. They all chattered about what song they could sing that Pete's family would know the words to and finally chose *Amazing Grace*. Cephas' family sang beautiful harmonies while Pete tried to fit in somewhere. Lisa and her daughters blended in nicely.

When Pete and Lisa finally lay down, he started to drift off right away. As he was falling asleep, he muttered, "Why didn't you help me get out of making hay tomorrow?"

"We couldn't just tell them we didn't want to help Marcus's family make hay; that would be rude," Lisa said.

"Are you kidding? We are paying these people good money to help them do all their work!"

"Shush," Lisa scolded. "Do you want them to hear us? Don't you know all the windows are open? They can probably hear every word we say. And besides, they seem to enjoy their work. I don't think they are trying to use us."

"They don't know any other life. This hard work is all they've ever known," Pete said.

"Yes, if they knew how good our life in town is, they would want to trade places with us for sure," Lisa said, her voice heavy with sarcasm.

"I'm too tired to fight about it," Pete groaned.

"Maybe that is why Amish people don't get divorced; they are too tired to fight," Lisa said with a giggle. They laughed together until Lisa said, "Shhh, they are going to hear us." Pete dozed off to sleep and then woke up because the bed was shaking. He realized Lisa was still trying unsuccessfully to hold back giggles about her own humorous comment.

Another Fine Day

Morning light glimmered through the open window. Robins began a soft song, and a horse whinnied in the distance. Pete jumped up. "Oh no, I must have slept in."

"It's only 5:30," Lisa whispered as she looked at her watch.

"Huh, I must be getting used to this lifestyle."

Pete pulled on his broadfall pants, and Lisa tied her apron over her Amish dress. They stepped out of their room, and Dory smiled at them. "I was going to let you sleep in a little longer, but I see you are ready to start your day."

"I guess we are getting used to it," Lisa said. "What can I do to help this morning?" Pete heard Lisa offer, as he headed out the door.

Pete stopped to watch Natalie and her friends feeding bottle calves.

"Dad, take hold of this bottle for a moment." Natalie moved her hands enough that Pete could take hold. The baby cow almost pulled it out of his hands.

"Wow, those little babies mean business, don't they?" Pete said.

"I wish we could have a calf."

"They don't allow that in Chicago," Pete answered.

"Then we need to move," she said seriously.

Pete smiled and passed the bottle back to his daughter and

headed into the big barn.

***

"Breakfast was delicious again," Pete said.

"Your wife helped make it," Dory replied, and she and Lisa met eyes and smiled.

Pete took another piece of homemade bread and doused it with strawberry jam. "We are getting our money's worth in food, with all of this great cooking," Pete said.

Lisa gave him a sharp glance as though she didn't like him bringing up the money topic.

"I should hope you are," Cephas quipped.

"Lisa told us a little about her work as a nurse at the Children's Hospital, while we were making breakfast," Dory said.

"She didn't tell you details and sad facts about sick children, did she?" Pete looked at his wife and raised his eyebrows.

"She just told us some cute stories about some sweet things children say," Dory told Pete.

Lisa gave her husband a knowing look and a smile.

***

By the time Cephas' and Pete's family met Marcus in his hayfield, they could see a large crew of girls making hay in Amish dresses of different colors. They all worked hard throwing bales, just as they had done the day before. Marcus was much friendlier than Cephas. He gave Pete tips on how to use momentum to swing bales without hurting his back.

"If our hayrack is heading uphill, that is a good time to stack bales higher, because the back of the hayrack is actually downhill."

"Huh, I never thought of that," Pete said.

During most of the day, Pete was stuck inside a hot barn

with Cephas' sons, stacking hay again. Now and then he and the boys stepped outside for a breath of fresh air. Amish girls in a whole variety of colorful dresses could be seen out in Marcus' hayfield. Pete tried to see if he could tell which were his daughters but couldn't. On one of his short breaks, Natalie quietly took her dad's hand and pulled him out behind the big barn.

"Where are you taking me?" Pete asked.

"You have to see these baby horses!"

She led her dad around the far side of the barn to a small pasture with three huge draft horses, each with a foal at her side. Natalie climbed the gate and started walking toward one of the giant mamas.

"Natalie, what are you doing? Those mama horses may get protective and come after you!"

"It's okay, Dad. I've been out here several times already today. These big horses are super gentle."

Pete climbed over the gate and walked close to one of the big mares. She calmly continued her grazing while he ran a hand along her warm side. Her foal moved close and seemed as curious about the humans as they were about the horses. Natalie stood near her dad and laughed as the foal reached its nose in and nibbled her dress. Natalie reached her hand out to pet the baby, but it retracted its nose just beyond her fingertips.

"Aren't they so cute?" Natalie said and looked at her dad.

"They sure are, but you better be careful. These older horses don't seem mean at all, but they are big enough they could accidentally hurt each other or one of us."

"I guess that's what happens with human parents, too," Natalie said.

"What do you mean?"

"Well, you and Mom are both really nice, but sometimes you accidentally hurt each other."

"What? What do you mean by that?"

"Like the time you and Mom were moving the couch

upstairs, and you pinched Mom's fingers against the banister," Natalie said.

"That wasn't my fault; she should have been paying more attention." He looked at his daughter, and her brown eyes met his.

"She told me that her feelings were hurt more than her hand," Natalie said.

"What did she say?"

"She said it would have been nice if you had said that you were sorry, instead of yelling at her for not being careful." Before Pete could make a comment, he saw Lisa standing by the fence.

"Oh, these babies are cute, aren't they," she called.

The three small Belgian colts near Pete and Natalie continued nosing at them and playfully nipping at each other.

"Yeah, they are, but Natalie and I better get out of here before their play fighting gets rough," Pete hollered back.

He took Natalie's hand and led her in a wide circle around the foals. The babies galloped away, kicking at each other as they ran. Lisa watched from beyond the fence with a big smile.

"Doesn't Mom look pretty in Amish clothes?" Natalie whispered to her dad.

"Yes," Pete answered and smiled at his daughter. Natalie looked at her dad in the eyes and grinned. Pete worried that Natalie was getting her hopes up and didn't want to see her disappointed, so he added. "Mom will go back to her makeup and jeans as soon as we leave here, though."

"She is pretty in those things, too, don't you think?"

Pete coughed and cleared his throat before answering quietly. "Yes, but these Amish clothes seem to soften her somehow."

After he had said it, he wondered if it was too much to say to his young daughter. They both looked across the field at Lisa, who was waiting for them at the gate with a big smile. As they walked toward her, Natalie whispered, "Yeah, you are right."

***

While they were riding home from Marcus' farm to Cephas', Pete said, "Tonight our family would like to head into town for supper."

"That would be fine with us," Cephas answered.

"Dad, would it be okay if I don't go with you?" Carrie called from the back of the hayrack. "Marcus' daughters invited me to go along to a volleyball game. All the teens from their church are getting together for the evening, and I really want to go along."

"Oh, that sounds fun," Lisa said.

"Could I stay here, too?" Natalie piped up. "We want to ride ponies this evening." Pete looked back and saw Natalie's smile and pleading eyes.

"I guess it'll just be me and Lisa going out for supper," Pete said.

"We don't need to go if the children aren't going," Lisa said quietly.

"I've got an idea," Dory interjected. "You two should take a picnic basket and have some quiet time together down by our creek. There is a beautiful spot down in our pasture where we like to have picnics. When we get back to the house, I'll put together a basket for you to take."

"You don't need to do that," Pete said.

"No, that wouldn't be necessary," Lisa agreed.

"Really, it's no problem," Dory said. "We want you to have time alone. It's good for a husband and wife to spend a little time together every now and then."

"Huh, we never thought of that," Lisa said under her breath.

6

Romance?

As they were finishing up evening chores, Jonas appeared in the milk house. "Come with me, Pete," he instructed. "I harnessed up Lady and Manny and hitched them to a wagon. You can drive them down along the edge of this cornfield." Jonas pointed to a lane which ran along the edge of a tall stand of rich-green cornstalks. "At the bottom of a low area, you will come to a gate. Our horses will go through when you swing it open. Call *whoa* to them when they are far enough through to shut the gate, and they will wait for you to get back in the wagon."

Old Jonas looked at Pete to see if he understood the directions. Pete nodded, and Jonas continued. "Keep following that lane on around a grove of trees, and you will see an open area with a picnic table. Take the opportunity to visit with your wife about her interests."

Pete gave Jonas a funny look. "I don't even know what those are," he said.

"This will be a good time to find out," Jonas answered with a smile.

Pete drove the wagon up near the house and found Lisa standing at the end of the sidewalk with a picnic basket in her hands. Carrie and her teenage Amish friends were climbing into a buggy. They called "Have fun" as they waved good-byes and headed out of the long lane. Natalie and the little girls rode past them on ponies. Their little mounts were all trotting, and the children looked as if they were about to jiggle off.

Lisa handed up her picnic basket, and Pete set it carefully inside the wagon. He had to take her hand to help her up, and it was soft and small in his. He wondered when he had last held her hand. She sat beside him on the wagon seat and asked, "Do you know how to drive these huge horses?"

"Not really; maybe we should ask Cephas and Dory to come with us."

"You'll be fine," a voice said from behind them. They hadn't noticed Jonas come up. "Lady and Manny are good horses and will do whatever you ask. Take your time and if you get nervous just say, 'Whoa.' They will stop in their tracks and wait for you to decide what to do next."

"Okay," Pete said without confidence. Jonas made a clucking noise, and the horses moved out. After Pete had directed them to the lane along the cornfield, the horses seemed to know where they were headed. They followed along a shady lane next to growing rows of corn. A woven-wire fence ran along the other side of the lane. Trees lined the pasture beyond. The grass, apparently grazed short by cattle and horses, looked as well-mown as a golf course. Birds sang sweetly. Lisa smiled as she and her husband made their way toward the gate.

"Who would have ever thought we would do something like this," Lisa said.

"Yeah, I have to say this Amish Park is amazing. I'm surprised they expect us to work so much but it is worth every penny. I'm going to recommend it to my friends at the office, but I'm not telling them how early the Amish get up." They both laughed.

Pete got out of the wagon to open the gate, and Lisa's face turned white.

"Don't leave me in here alone with these horses," she said.

Pete grinned and opened the gate. Lady and Manny stepped

through the opening. Lisa gasped and put her hands on her cheeks.

"Stop them, Pete, they are going to run off!"

Pete calmly called, "Whoa." Both large horses stopped instantly.

"Don't scare me like that, I thought they might run off," Lisa scolded with a smile on her face.

Pete laughed and climbed back into the wagon. He clucked, and his team of horses continued around a grove of trees and out into an open area.

Everything was exactly like Jonas had described, including the picnic table near the creek. The hitching rack was not far away, perfectly placed under a shade tree. Pete tied the horses, and Lisa placed her picnic basket on the table. She pulled out a table cloth, plates, glasses, and silverware.

"Dory helped me put together a meal," Lisa said. She seemed to be blushing as she set a vase on the table with flowers in it. Pete watched her, surprised at how pretty she looked in an Amish dress and head scarf. When everything was ready, they took seats on opposite sides, facing each other.

"I guess we should put our hands down and pray," Pete said.

Lisa smiled and bowed her head. Pete had been joking, but when she bowed her head, he did the same and prayed in his heart. *"Help me Lord; I have no idea what to say to this woman."* He cleared his throat, and she looked up. They met eyes briefly and looked away awkwardly. The stream gurgled gently in the background and made things uncomfortably romantic.

Lisa talked as she handed out the food, explaining how Dory had prepared everything. She filled the awkward silence by telling all about Dory's garden and what was growing in it.

"Our daughters seem to be having a lot of fun," Lisa stated.

"I knew Natalie would like it," Pete said. "But I'm really surprised that Carrie is enjoying herself."

"I know!" Lisa looked right at Pete and gave him a surprised expression. "I haven't seen her this happy for years! She doesn't complain about working in the garden and gets up every morning and hurries out to milk cows."

"Cephas' and Marcus' daughters are a great influence on her, I guess," Pete said. They both laughed and ate more of the delicious garden produce. "I love this tea they make," Pete said after a long, refreshing gulp of garden tea.

"They raise it in their garden. Dory is planning to send a start of it for us to plant in our back yard. She already taught me how to make it."

Everything got quiet again, and they listened to the sound of water bubbling over rocks. A few birds sang in branches overhead, trying their best to make a cheery mood. Pete finished eating what was on his plate.

"I guess we can head back now?" Lisa said.

Pete stood up and helped her clear off the table and put everything back into their wagon. He thought about what Jonas had suggested. He was afraid the old man may ask him what happened and be disappointed if he didn't follow up with his advice.

"Let's go down and look at the water," Pete said, trying to sound casual.

"Okay," Lisa whispered.

The brook was beautiful. Clear water flowed over smooth, moss-covered rocks. Both banks were mown short by grazing livestock, offering a park-like feel which was heavenly.

"I'm going to take off my shoes and wade in this creek. I haven't done that since I was a boy," Pete said.

He sat on the grass and pulled off his shoes and socks. Lisa watched with a smile on her face while he cuffed up his pants. He stepped down the short bank and into the water.

"Ooh, this water is nice and cool; you need to sit on the edge and dangle your feet in too," Pete told her.

Lisa headed to the picnic table and took off her shoes and Amish stockings. She sat on the bank, dipping her feet into the cool water for a bit.

"Here," Pete said. "Take my hand and step in with me."

She took his hand, and her smile reminded him of Natalie's. Pete had a fleeting thought; his wife had been a little girl not so many years ago and probably looked a lot like his daughter.

"Oh, this does feel good. The rocks all have a silky moss on them, and it makes everything soft to walk on," Lisa said.

"Yeah, but it makes it a little slick, too," Pete added.

Lisa started to slip and let out a giggle. Pete caught her, almost holding her in his arms.

"Whew, that was close!" She barely got the words out, and they both went down with a splash, and both came up laughing.

"I'm glad I didn't have my cellphone on me," Pete said.

Lisa wrung out the bottom of her apron and asked, "What will Cephas and Dory think?"

"We'll just tell them the truth, we slipped and fell in the creek. Besides, I've been hot all day, and now, I'm finally comfortable. Maybe we should relax down here while our clothes dry out."

Lisa nodded and followed Pete to the picnic table, and they took seats again.

"So, what do you like to talk about?" Pete asked.

"What do you mean?"

"What are you interested in?" Pete said.

"Our daughters are my main interest, I guess. Why do you ask?"

"Er, I was just w… wondering," he stuttered.

"Oh, that's nice. I've always been interested in horticulture; that's why I spend so much time landscaping our yard."

"Huh, I thought you were trying to make it look better," Pete said.

"I do want it to look nice, but I enjoy planting seeds and watching things grow."

"Interesting," Pete said and meant it. "This is a good vacation spot for you then, being out on the farm with a big garden."

"Yes, it is. I've learned a lot from Dory already. She is a great gardener and has all kinds of advice for me. Carrie has the same interest in gardening. She has been super inquisitive about everything Dory teaches us."

"I never would have known that about either of you," Pete said.

"Maybe if you spent more time at home, you would know a little more about your daughters," she answered quietly.

"Maybe if you weren't so grouchy all the time, I'd feel like coming home!" he said.

"Please, don't start yelling again," she whispered.

"Oh great, it's all my fault. You always make it out like all of our troubles are my fault!"

"Can we go back now? I'm starting to get cold," Lisa said. She hugged herself and began to shiver.

Pete headed over and untied the horses. He climbed in and didn't offer his wife any help when she struggled to get up into the wagon. They rode up the beautiful lane in silence. Everything around them seemed so peaceful and sweet it almost made him angry. In town, when he was in a bad mood, he could be frustrated about traffic lights or honk at other motorists.

When Lady and Manny were asked to stop at the gate, they did exactly as they were told. Pete gave them a go-ahead cluck, and they moved up. He called 'whoa' in a grouchy way, and they stopped obediently.

"Don't take it out on the horses; they didn't do anything wrong," Lisa muttered.

Pete pretended he didn't hear her.

He didn't drive Lisa close to the house, but stopped halfway to the barn and said, "Do you want out now?" She struggled to get out of the wagon and had a little trouble getting her picnic basket. He sat without words and didn't offer to help her.

Pete drove his horses near the barn and tried to unhook

them. Old Jonas came out of the grandpa house and helped. He showed his visitor how to remove the harness, and they brushed the horses.

"So, how did it go down by the creek?" Jonas asked with a friendly smile.

"We were having a good time; I took your advice and asked Lisa about her interests. Then, all at once we started arguing. I don't even remember how it started."

Jonas pulled on his beard for a few moments, then said, "You made a start in the right direction. Tomorrow is a new day; the mercies of the Lord are new every morning."

Pete didn't know how to respond to that; he just said "Thanks" and headed for the house. Jonas went back to his grandpa house.

As soon as Pete heard Jonas' door shut, he did a U-turn. He didn't feel like going inside right away and facing Lisa again. He decided to take a short walk in the darkness and headed out into Cephas' hayfield. Everything was quiet, except for the sound of crickets and bullfrogs. Great hordes of fireflies lit up over the empty field. He stood for a long time and watched them flash on and off. He made a fist and spoke to Cephas' farm.

"Don't try to change me! In a couple of days, we are going back to Chicago and real life! I've had about all I can take out of this Cephas charging us money to do his work and then treating us like we are in the way. Lisa acts all sweet in an Amish dress, but when she puts back on her pants, she'll be right back to her old ways!"

Pete looked up toward the grandpa house to be sure he was far enough into the hayfield that Jonas couldn't hear him.

"I can't believe how mean-hearted that woman is — to start a fight when I was trying to be nice."

While he was standing in the darkness, he heard a horse trotting into the lane. He watched from his hiding place under a maple tree as the young people climbed out of the buggy.

Carrie and Ada chattered about the fun they had during the evening as they helped James take his horse away from the buggy and lead it toward the barn. Pete thought it would be a good moment to step inside before they saw him lurking around in the darkness. He almost made it to the house before he realized Carrie was only a few yards in front of him looking at Dory's garden by starlight.

Pete cleared his throat to keep from scaring his daughter when he spoke. "After playing Amish volleyball, you are probably ready to leave this place?"

"No, actually it was really fun! It wasn't like high school volleyball, but I liked it better. It wasn't so competitive. Instead, we just had fun. Everyone was friendly and made me feel welcome. At my school, the girls are so mean you need to be super careful what you say or do, or they kick you out of the popular group."

Pete looked at his daughter with renewed compassion. Maybe that was why she was so grouchy and on edge all the time. He had never imagined she was under that kind of pressure. He wanted to keep the conversation going because she usually didn't confide in him at all. Pete tried to think of another topic.

"I know that James isn't like the guys at your high school, but he is a nice young man and fun to be around, isn't he?"

Carrie gave her dad a sideways look as if she didn't know what he was trying to say.

"James seems nice enough to me, even if he is a bit old-fashioned," Pete tried to explain. Lantern light glowed out of the kitchen window just enough so that he could see his daughters face.

Carrie rolled her eyes and stated emphatically, "Seriously, he is dreamy!"

"Are you being sarcastic?" Pete asked.

"No, I mean it." She smiled with the look a teenage girl gives when infatuated with a young man. Then she added, "James is so good-looking and polite. He's everything a girl my age finds attractive in a guy!"

"Really?" Pete was caught off guard. He thought James seemed like a very nice young man; however, Carrie's reaction was the last thing he expected.

Carrie pointed to the garden and said, "I think I've discovered what I really enjoy doing."

"What is that?" Pete asked.

"Gardening. I think I want to study horticulture in college. Mom and I both love gardening."

"Huh, I didn't know. Does Natalie share your interest too?"

"No, Natalie likes to cook and bake," she said.

Cephas' teenage daughters came walking toward them, so Pete headed inside. He slipped into his bedroom and found that the lantern was already blown out. He was relieved that he didn't have to try to talk to Lisa. As he crawled into bed, he made every effort not to wake her. He got comfortable and was enjoying the night sounds coming in through the window screen. A gentle breeze caused the curtains to move slightly, as a scent of flowers and hay drifted through the room.

Pete heard a noise he couldn't place at first. Then, he realized the sound was coming from his wife beside him. He concluded that Lisa was crying, with her face buried in a pillow to keep him from hearing her sobs.

7

Stubborn

A soft knock at the door woke up Pete. The bed shook as Lisa stood up and got ready for chores. "Pete, they tapped on the door. It's time for morning chores."

"I'm not ready to get up, yet," Pete said, and pulled the sheet over his head to keep morning light out of his eyes.

"I overheard Cephas tell Dory that you aren't pulling your weight," Lisa whispered.

Pete sat up and threw the covers off. "That does it; I'm going to tell that guy off!"

Lisa motioned for her husband to calm down and whispered, "Please, for our daughters' sake, don't say anything."

Pete laid back on the bed and pulled the sheet back over his face. "I would have told him off already, but I like that old Jonas."

Lisa didn't say anything. Pete heard her shut the door as she walked out. He could hear Dory mention his name and his wife quietly responded, "Pete isn't feeling well this morning."

He lay still, trying to fall back to sleep, but he couldn't. Instead, he listened to Lisa's voice, yet couldn't make out her words. Dory's voice alternated with Lisa's for a long stretch of time. Pete imagined Lisa was telling Dory what a terrible husband he was and that Dory was trying to console her. Pete sat up and worked hard to hear what Lisa was saying.

"I've not been a very good wife. I work in the children's hospital as a nurse, and I know I get too involved in the lives of my patients. Instead of coming home and being a happy, supportive wife, I get down and stress about my little sick children and their families. Pete tries to talk about his company and financial issues, and I struggle to focus. After watching families battle against illness, disabilities, and even death, money just doesn't seem like that big of a deal. If I try to talk to Pete about what is going on at work, he just tells me, 'You need to be more professional. You can't let yourself get so involved with your patients and their families.' I know he's right, but I can't help it."

Their conversation ended, and kitchen sounds continued as the women prepared a large breakfast. Dory began singing a hymn, and after one verse, Lisa's voice chimed in, singing along. Just as Pete finally dozed off, he heard Lisa open the door.

"Are you going to come out for breakfast?" she asked quietly.

He didn't answer, but sat on the edge of the bed and started getting dressed.

During breakfast, everyone talked cheerfully, except Pete and Cephas.

"We had lots of fun riding ponies while you were on a picnic," Natalie said enthusiastically.

"You should have seen your daughter ride," Ida told them. "Our old pony, Cob, goes out of his way to do whatever she asks of him."

"He's the best pony ever!" Natalie's face was glowing brighter than a lantern. "Cob is so easy to ride, and he doesn't go over jumps."

"Is that good, that he doesn't go over jumps?" Pete asked.

"It is for me," Natalie said. "The others all rode their ponies over jumps, but I didn't want to. Cob was perfect for me because he doesn't like jumps either. He just ran around all the obstacles." Everyone laughed.

"Carrie fit right in with our young folks last night, too," Ada said.

"Yeah, she's really good at volleyball," James added. "She can really jump and spike the ball!"

"Did I look like I was trying too hard?" Carrie asked.

"No, everyone liked you," Ada said.

"Yeah, we all were glad you were there," James agreed.

Dory looked at Pete and asked, "Do you like the coffee cake?"

"Mmm yeah," he tried to answer with a mouthful of amazingly soft and sweet coffee cake.

"Your daughter, Natalie, made that cake," Dory said.

"You made this coffee cake?" Pete asked, with wide eyes.

Natalie smiled shyly and answered, "Dory helped me."

Cephas spoke up. "The way you are eating, you must be feeling better?"

Pete looked at him and opened his mouth to tell him off. He could see little Natalie out of the corner of his eye and changed his mind. Instead of telling Cephas what he wanted to say, Pete said, "Yeah, I'm feeling a little better."

"Good," Cephas said, "We have plenty of work that needs done around here."

Pete could feel his face heat up. He looked across the table at his daughters; they were both staring at him wide-eyed. He instantly knew they were fully expecting him to start yelling, as he usually did when confronted. Pete forced himself to keep quiet by stuffing his mouth with another bite of Natalie's amazing coffee cake. Cephas cleared his throat, and everyone knew it was a signal for silent prayer. Pete prayed silently, *"Lord, help me. I feel like I'm about to explode."*

Pete followed Cephas outside, and they met up with Jonas near the horse barn. He was happy to see the friendly older man. He smiled at Jonas, but inside, he was planning to find a moment alone with Cephas to tell him what he really thought.

"I'm glad you are feeling better, Pete," Jonas said. "I prayed for you when I heard you weren't well."

"Thank you. I guess I'm just not used to all of this heat and hard work."

"It's about time you gave it a try," Cephas teased.

Pete felt his temper rising again, but Jonas' kind eyes met his. The older man looked at his son and spoke. "You know Cephas, we would probably find life in town to be difficult. I'm sure after a long day in a stuffy office and fighting traffic on the highway, we would be at our wit's end, too."

The men harnessed Lady and Manny in silence. Finally, old Jonas spoke, "We are going to pick up rocks today."

"What does that mean?" Pete asked.

"Just what he said, 'Pick up rocks,'" Cephas answered.

Jonas and Cephas hitched their huge blond horses onto a flat sled and climbed aboard. They motioned for Pete to join them. He barely got his feet on the sled before Cephas kissed to his horses, sending them off with a jerk. Pete raised his arms like a surfboarder to keep his balance without holding onto the other men. Jonas stood like a rock.

"Our fields have some stones in them," Jonas said. "Every year we take a pass over our farm and pick up whatever has risen to the surface. We noticed some big ones while making hay and thought we should get them out."

Pete smiled at Jonas to let him know he appreciated the explanation.

Jonas added, "In the spring, we usually have the children pick up rocks, but this year we noticed some bigger ones that may need men and horses to get out."

They rode out along a fence row until they were at the far end of the field. Cephas called "whoa," and his horses stood still. Jonas scrounged a shovel off the sled and began digging at what looked like a small flat rock. In a short time, the older man moved enough dirt to expose part of a boulder. Cephas pushed a long pry-bar in alongside the hole Jonas was digging and wiggled it.

"Jonas, please let me dig for a while; that is something I think I can handle," Pete said.

Jonas smiled as he handed over his shovel, and Pete began digging. When Pete looked up next, he saw that Jonas had unhooked his horses from the sled and had them backed up near the rock. Cephas wrapped a chain around a narrow place on the boulder, and Jonas spoke softly to his horses.

"Lady, Manny, ease up there, ease up there." Both horses moved ahead slowly until the chain between their double-tree and the rock was tight. Pete didn't see or hear anything from old Jonas; however, as though the horses had read his mind, they slowly crouched and arched their necks. Muscles rippled through their hind quarters down to their hocks. The boulder moved from its foundation ever so slightly, and Jonas said a quiet "Whoa." Both horses relaxed and stood still.

"There, we jarred it loose. Pete, go ahead and dig down on the other side of that stone," Jonas instructed.

Pete did as he was told while Jonas repositioned his horses on the opposite side of the hole. Cephas wrapped the chain and hooked it tight again. Jonas eased his horses forward, and they began to crouch and arch their massive necks. This time the boulder had more room and tilted until it came against the slope Pete had dug into the ground. Jonas spoke a low command, and his horses powered forward with a surge. The chain clunked and thumped. Pete could feel the earth rumble as the horses heaved the boulder up out of the soil where it had been buried since the beginning of time. Jonas gave another softly spoken "Whoa." His horses lifted their heads and relaxed again.

"Do you see how good Lady and Manny work together?" Jonas asked. "That steel contraption they are hooked to is called an evener. It's designed to help two horses share a load. It has some give so that if one horse stumbles, the other horse can carry the load until their teammate regains their footing. Also, one horse is usually stronger than the other, and the evener allows them to do their best together. An interesting fact; two horses hitched as a team can pull more than double what one horse can pull by itself."

"I wonder why that would be?" Pete asked.

"It could be that they are able to keep the momentum better because if one hesitates, the other keeps things moving. Or, maybe it's just the motivation they get from each other. We all feel better when we have someone helping us."

Pete stood and looked at the evener and thought about what Jonas was saying until he heard Cephas' voice. "I'm going to walk this fence here and check on my cows."

"That sounds good," Jonas said. "We'll head on over to the next stone."

As Cephas walked away, Pete helped Jonas hitch his horses back onto the sled. "You can drive them across the field if you want," Jonas said.

"Okay, I'd like that," Pete answered as he took the driving lines and clucked to Lady and Manny. Pete watched how well they cooperated to pull the sled which now had a heavy boulder and two men riding onboard. Jonas pointed forward between the horses.

"That small wooden pole between them is called a neck-yoke. A neck-yoke makes it possible for Manny and Lady to pull a wagon together. The tongue is held up between them, and their movement guides the direction of the wheels or sled. When they back up, they need to cooperate with their master. All three of them work together to step back, and then they can re-start in a better direction." Pete listened to Jonas carefully. He was just thinking that Jonas may be trying to teach him something about husbands and wives when Jonas spoke again.

"Is there anything you have done to hurt your wife or failed to do?"

"Maybe? But I think I'm doing a lot of things right, and she doesn't appreciate me."

Jonas scratched his beard in thought while Pete waited. Finally, Jonas continued. "If you are in your car, speeding down the highway and a policeman pulls you over for breaking a law, he doesn't compliment you for what you had been doing right, does he?"

Pete looked at his feet and shook his head.

Jonas continued. "Even if you were doing a lot of things right, he won't thank you for that. He will address what you did wrong. The same is true with your wife. You are not doing your wife a favor when you do your part as a husband and a father. That is what you should do."

Pete met Jonas' eyes and took note of the old man's kind face, wrinkled with age.

Jonas smiled and said, "True, it is nice when people appreciate our efforts. Unfortunately, the few things we let go, or do wrong, overshadow all the good things we are trying to do. If you address your failures, you will be surprised at how quickly your wife will begin to appreciate the good things you do. But, for now, those dark areas are all she can feel or see."

Cephas came back, and they started working on the next rock. This time Pete started digging around what he could see of the stone while Cephas used his pry bar. In a short time, they had pushed it out of the ground without having to use the horses.

"Well, that stone was smaller than I expected," Pete said.

"Certain things in life are like that. What is on the surface doesn't always reveal what is unseen," Jonas replied.

The dinner bell rang, and Cephas said, "We can finish digging out rocks this afternoon."

***

After lunch, Pete and Lisa stepped into their room for a few moments. Pete didn't plan to talk, but Lisa asked, "You didn't say anything to Cephas, did you?"

"No, Jonas was right there with us, or I would have."

"You aren't going to tell him off for charging us money and making us work, are you?" she asked.

"Nope, I'm going to congratulate him on how ingenious his business model is."

"What do you mean?" Lisa asked.

"I'm going to come up with a business where I can charge people money to do my work. Maybe I'll start a business for Amish people. *'Come see how us English people live. You will only need to work eight hours in a factory. After that, you can go out for supper and still have enough energy left over to watch TV and fight with your wife in the evenings.'*" He looked at Lisa for the first time since their picnic.

She put her finger up to her mouth to shush him.

"I'm tired of being quiet!" he said, his voice getting louder.

Lisa covered her face and began to cry again. Pete stomped out of their room and headed out to the barn even though the others were still inside. He stood and looked at Lady and Manny as they munched on hay. He was feeling bad about making Lisa cry, and he remembered hearing her sobs in bed the night before.

Pete walked into Manny's stall and stood next to the massive horse and whispered to him. "How do you do it? How do you stay calm and work so well with Lady? I try to get along with Lisa, but she always finds a way to set off my temper." He smoothed his hand over Manny's huge neck and admired his size and power. He heard footsteps and realized that Cephas had come back into the barn by himself.

"Jonas will be out in a few moments; he told me that he needed to run up to the phone booth and make a quick call," Cephas said.

Pete instantly thought about his plans to tell Cephas what he thought. He would have at that very moment if he hadn't just made Lisa cry. He tried to bite his tongue and not talk at all.

"We can go ahead and hitch Lady and Manny to the sled. Do you want to drive them out?" Cephas asked.

"Sure," Pete said. He untied the big horses and pulled their driving lines from Lady's harness and backed them out of their stall. He drove them over to the sled, and Manny stepped obediently over the tongue and stood waiting to be hitched. Pete watched the horses with awe. He was surprised at himself that he was driving such an impressive set of animals. The men stepped onto the stone-boat and headed out toward the hayfield without speaking to each other. Driving horses kept Pete's mind occupied. Cephas directed where they needed to go to find the next large stone that needed to be removed.

As soon as they reached the spot, Pete stepped off the sled with a shovel and started digging near the rock. Cephas wielded his pry bar and shoved it deep in the hole.

"Here, dig a little on this side," Cephas ordered.

Pete complied, but he felt his temper rise. He was just getting going when Cephas reached over and took the shovel out of his hands.

"It works better if you do it like this," Cephas said.

Pete put his hands on his hips and opened his mouth to spew out a few choice words when he heard Jonas' voice.

"It looks like you two are getting along pretty good. The phone booth is just beyond those trees over there, so I thought I'd meet you out here in the field."

They all took turns digging. Finally, Jonas backed his horses to the boulder, and Cephas hooked the chain. Jonas asked his horses quietly, "Step up." The both obediently moved forward until their heel chains were snug. Both horses were snorting and prancing, anticipating what was coming next. Their ears twitched as they listened for a command from Jonas. He calmly said, "Get up." Lady and Manny threw all their weight into the thick leather collars on their shoulders.

Pete watched with awe as the horses blew and snorted. They crouched low, and Manny let out a low groan. At that very moment, the earth shook, and the chain clunked. A dirty boulder climbed out of its hiding place and lay exposed to the bright afternoon sun. "Whoa," Jonas said. His horses stood and relaxed, taking in deep breaths.

The three men and huge horses headed to their next hidden obstacle. This boulder looked like it would be easy to dig out at first. It had a smaller section on top; but as they continued digging, they found it too big to pull even with horses.

"We'd better set up a post near this one and leave it alone. We will need to farm around it, or hire someone with a caterpillar to dig it out," Cephas said.

Pete drove Lady and Manny back to the barn.

"I'm going to go check on my heifers in that far lot over yonder," Cephas told them. Jonas and Pete watched him walk away; afterward, they stood in silence for a while.

The Lesson

"I believe that a man should be the leader in his home," Jonas said matter-of-factly.

"I can't be, because my wife doesn't listen to me." Pete chuckled out of awkwardness.

"When you look at our horses, can you tell which is the lead horse?" Jonas asked.

"I'm gonna guess, Manny?" Pete said.

"Why do you think I always put him in a hitch as the lead horse?"

"Oh, I don't know… because he is the strongest?" Pete looked at old Jonas, to see if he answered right. Jonas didn't speak but stood looking at his big horse. He walked over and adjusted Manny's harness and smoothed a hand over his thick neck.

"This may surprise you, but I use Manny as the lead horse because he is very humble."

"Humble?" Pete looked to see if Jonas was joking. "How can a horse be humble?"

"He does whatever I ask of him and doesn't question his master. When he is asked to turn, he turns. When he is asked to stop, he stops." Jonas looked Pete in the eyes as if reading to see if his point were being understood. The old Amish man leaned against the huge side of his horse and said, "I used to think being the leader of the home meant that I should tell everyone else what to do. I learned something from my horses. A good leader leads by being a good example, by serving his master." Jonas looked at Pete intently.

"I'm just not getting it; what do you mean?" Pete said.

"Being a leader means that you should be the first one to say, 'I'm sorry; I was wrong.'"

"If I say that to Lisa, then she will win, and then she will be the leader of our home."

Jonas shook his head. "You and your wife are a team; if she wins, you win." The old Amish man bent down and picked a small flower that was growing near the fence. He handed it to Pete and said, "Take this flower to your wife. When you hand it to her, tell her you are sorry."

"For what?" Pete asked.

"I'm guessing she has already told you. You think about what she tells you she doesn't like. Give her the flower and tell her that she is right, and you are sorry." Jonas walked away after those words. Pete stood there, looking at the tiny flower Jonas had put into his hand. He asked himself: *What does Lisa say she doesn't like?* Instantly, Pete knew. He slowly walked into the big house, hoping something else would be going on, preventing him from talking to Lisa. As soon as he walked in, Dory spoke.

"Lisa just stepped into her room for a short nap."

"Oh, I'd better not bother her." Pete sighed with relief.

"She only stepped in a few minutes ago; I'm sure she won't mind."

Pete opened the door; it creaked slightly. Lisa was sitting on the edge of the bed taking the scarf off her head. Her black bun looked cute with her Amish dress. Pete tried to hide the little flower when she looked at him.

"What do you have there?" she asked.

"I brought this little flower to give to you," he forced himself to say.

"Oh, that is so sweet." She took it with a smile and held it to her nose, breathing in deeply. Pete was surprised she didn't think it was dumb. He knew what he was supposed to do next. However, he doubted Jonas was right about letting Lisa win their marriage-long fight. She looked at him with her pretty, dark eyes as though trying to figure out why he was standing there dumbfounded. At the last second, he decided he had nothing to lose; he forced the words out.

"Lisa, I'm sorry I yell all the time." As the words left his mouth, tears came to his eyes.

Lisa stood up as if completely shocked at what was happening. She looked at his tears and reached out and hugged him tightly.

He said it again. "I'm so sorry, Lisa, please forgive me." He tried to stop his tears, but they kept flowing.

She held him tightly and spoke softly. "No, it's my fault. If I would only try to listen to you, you wouldn't feel like you need to yell. Please forgive me." As she said the words, he felt her body shake with sobs.

After they held each other and cried for a time unknown to them, Lisa sat on the edge of the bed as though worn out. Pete looked into her dark eyes. "Please, Hun, let's not get a divorce, let's try starting over again."

She held his hands and nodded as tears continued to stream down her cheeks. He sat beside her and held her hand until she fell asleep. Lisa's breathing was long and deep. Pete watched her pretty face for a while, but he couldn't wait to talk to Jonas and thank him. He stood up quietly, slipped out through the doorway and headed out to find the old man.

Jonas was in the barn feeding his horses. The older man spoke first.

"How did it go?"

Pete tried to make words come out, but he couldn't speak. He took off his straw hat and held it in his hands and looked at his feet. Jonas came over and put a hand on Pete's shoulder. "You did it, didn't you?" Pete nodded his head and looked up for a moment. Jonas' eyes were welling up with tears. "Good job, Pete, you will never be sorry you let her win. Now you will be a winning team, together, and your whole family will succeed."

"I think I need to have a similar conversation with the Lord," Pete said. He looked up at Jonas and asked, "Do you think it's the same with God as it is with my wife?"

"Well, it is very similar. We humans sometimes assume God will be happy if we do most things right, but think about how silly that is. Even if you were good enough to do almost everything right, you would still be deserving of punishment for the things you did wrong." Jonas looked at Pete, and the younger man nodded that he understood. Jonas continued, "God sees everything. He knows you have done many things right in your life. But, if you have committed sin, then you are a lawbreaker and must be punished. God is so just; He cannot leave one sin unpunished. Yet, He is so kind that he took our punishment on himself, on the cross. If we confess our sins and ask Him to forgive us, then our sins are nailed to the cross. Otherwise, we must pay for what we have done, and the payment for sin is death. You must choose."

"I'm going to go have a conversation with God, like the one I had with my wife," Pete said. "You don't mind if I go up in your haymow, do you?"

"Please do. That would be the best use our haymow has ever been put to," Jonas said.

Pete climbed the ladder up into a large hayloft. The wooden structure reminded him of an ancient cathedral. Stacks of hay towered around him. He climbed a section where the bales were staggered like a huge stairway. When he was on top, he looked up at the latticework of barn boards that made up a ceiling. Columns of golden light shot through a set of windows at one end and beamed across the open area, landing on the bales Pete kneeled on.

He bowed down and opened his mouth to pray. "Dear

God, please forgive me, I'm a sinner..." was all he got out. He fell flat and cried until he had no tears left. When he sat up again, he looked toward the windows. That golden light was blinding, yet somehow warm and comforting. He knew there was much more he needed to say and pray about, but he also felt that for now, he had said enough. He felt completely new inside. He was sure that God had been every bit as forgiving as his wife and more.

Pete lay back on the hay and looked at the cathedral-like insides of the barn. Those golden rays shone above him. Millions of tiny dust particles swirled about in the columns of light like stars in the heavens. Pete watched with a smile on his face like a little child, seeing the world for the first time. He didn't move until the sun sank below the windowsill and the beams of light became less and less.

***

As Pete walked across the yard, he met up with Jonas again. The old man looked at Pete with eyes full of compassion and kindness. "I'd better show you something." He pulled a letter from his shirt pocket and handed it over. Pete immediately recognized his daughter's handwriting and read the words out loud.

> *Dear Amish People,*
>
> *My name is Natalie. We would like to come stay on an Amish farm June 15th for a week. My family is having some really bad days. My mom and dad are planning to get a divorce. My friend Elaine told me that her family went to stay at the Amish farm for a week and it made them all happy. Maybe if we could come and work on your farm for a week, our family will see what good families are like. My dad is a business man. My mom is pretty and a nurse. My older sister*

is mad at the whole world, and all she does is look at her phone. I am 10 years old, and I love horses. I hope this is enough info about us. I'm praying that after we come to your place, Mom and Dad will change their minds and not get a divorce.

I am sending an envelope with a stamp. Please send me a letter if you need to know more.

Your friend, Natalie Heller.

"Well, that's kind of embarrassing," Pete said. "She saw on your Amish Park website that you wanted information about our family. She is only ten."

"We are not part of Amish Park," Jonas said.

"Wait a minute, what are you saying?"

"We are just an ordinary Amish family. Your daughter's letter touched our hearts, and we decided we should try to help." Jonas looked at Pete with a very sincere face.

Pete took off his straw hat and scratched his head. "Do you mean to say that this is a private family farm ... and you didn't receive any money from Amish Park for our stay here?"

"No, we have no connection with Amish Park or any tourist company."

"Jonas, this whole thing was a huge mistake; we would never expect you to take in our family for a week. You didn't even know us!"

"I don't think it was a mistake." Jonas smiled and looked Pete in the eyes. "I think the Lord was behind it all."

Pete shook his head. "I think you are right about the Lord being behind this, but we are going to give you money for taking us in."

Jonas folded his arms and looked very determined as he declared. "This was a gift from the Lord to you and your family. It was an answer to Natalie's prayers. We have other family friends come and stay in our home from time to time, and your family has become our very dear friends. We won't take money from our guests."

Pete was speechless. He ran his fingers through his hair while trying to think of how to express his gratitude.

Jonas laughed and added. "Besides, you already paid Amish Park for the week, and I've heard they don't give refunds."

Jonas and Pete laughed as they walked up to the large farmhouse. Dory and Lisa were sitting on the porch swing and snapping string beans. Pete looked at his wife.

"Lisa, I just found out something really shocking." Lisa dropped her hands to her lap and focused on her husband, in obvious fear about what news Pete may have. "We are not at Amish Park." Lisa and Dory looked at each other.

"What are you saying?" Lisa asked.

Simultaneously, Dory said, "Did you think you were at Amish Park?"

Pete tried to answer them both. "We signed up to be guests at Amish Park. Natalie misaddressed a letter to Jonas' home, and they answered her letter with an invitation for us to come and stay on their private farm."

"We would never have moved in on your family like that. This has all been a terrible mistake," Lisa told Jonas.

"It was no mistake," Jonas spoke with quiet authority. "Children speak honestly. Your daughter Natalie didn't know what Amish Park would be like, and none of this is her fault. She prayed for her family, and God answered her prayer. We all had a good week. Let's just give thanks to the Lord for his providence."

Dory sputtered, obviously trying to squelch laughter. Pete and Jonas looked at her to see what was going on. Lisa was looking at her feet and shaking. After a moment, a belly laugh came out of Lisa, and she looked at Dory. The two women made eye contact and burst into laughter. By that time Cephas and Jonas' wife, Mattie, had joined them, watching the women laugh.

At last, Dory composed herself enough to choke out the words. "Lisa and I figured out the mistake yesterday. We didn't tell you because we knew how upset Pete would be about the whole thing." The group of adults all laughed until they were almost crying, which drew Carrie and the teenagers out to see what was going on.

Lisa tried to explain the mess to them. "Pete and I thought we were at a tourist resort called Amish Park this whole week. We discovered that there was a misunderstanding and we stayed all week on your private Amish farm!" The teenagers laughed harder than the adults had.

"We figured that out on Wednesday," Carrie admitted.

"What?" Lisa asked with a shocked expression.

Carrie looked a little nervous as she explained. "I said something to Ada, and she told me that Amish Park is a hundred miles from here. I told her that I better say something to my dad and mom; they would never be willing to impose on anyone like that. Your daughters made me promise not to say anything because we were having so much fun, we didn't want it to end."

All of them laughed, and a few were wiping tears from their eyes. The laughter echoed off the house and barns. Natalie, Ida, and the little children came up from the pasture in their little pony-cart.

"What's going on up here?" Natalie asked.

Pete looked at his little girl and said calmly, "Honey, when you sent the letter to Amish Park, you miss-addressed it. This isn't Amish Park after all."

Natalie answered with a straight face. "Oh, I know."

"How did you know that?"

"Well, there wasn't a sign over the driveway like Amish Park has on the website," she answered sincerely. Pete and Lisa exchanged a look of horror that their daughter admitted she knew the mistake from day one.

Pete questioned her further. "So, Natalie, you knew we were

at the wrong place and didn't tell us?"

"I wasn't sure at first," she said with a cute innocent face. "I asked Ida and Orpha during lunch the first day, and they told me that we weren't at Amish Park. But, we talked to their grandpa about it, and he told us not to say anything. He said, 'Adults worry about things too much; let's just keep this to ourselves.'"

Natalie and her little Amish friends didn't even crack a smile. They clucked to their pony, and it trotted off toward the barn. All the adults and teenagers looked at Jonas. He smiled and shrugged his shoulders.

Pete turned to Cephas and said, "Well, it looks like we were the only two that didn't figure out what was going on?"

"I guess it's because we are so much alike," Cephas said with a smile. They all roared with laughter.

"How did everyone know that we would have so much in common?" Pete asked.

"Because we have the same name," Cephas explained.

"No, we don't, unless your first name is actually Peter?"

"In the Bible, Peter is also called Cephas. Cephas means rock, and Peter is the Greek word for it. So, we have the same name, and they were right, we have a lot in common." Cephas looked Pete in the eye and added, "I have to admit, I thought it was a little odd that you brought your family into our home without offering money or even thanking us for taking you in. I misjudged you."

"I have to admit that I misjudged you as well," Pete said, "I couldn't understand why you would take strangers into your home for a few extra bucks. I was going to give you a piece of my mind before I left. Or, congratulate you on your slick business venture; charging us to do your work."

Everyone laughed. Pete and Cephas shook hands and smiled at each other for the first time.

"I just guessed that something like this had happened," Mattie said. "I mentioned it to Jonas, and he told me, 'This is from the Lord; that is all we need to know.'"

Lisa had tears rolling down her cheeks as she choked out the words. "We will never forget what you have done for our family."

"You all should come back for a visit again next summer," Dory said with a smile. Pete and Lisa nodded but were speechless.

"Would you please stay an extra day as our friends?" Cephas asked sincerely. "We would like to have you come visit Church with us." Pete and Lisa looked into each other's eyes for a moment and nodded.

"We'd love to," Lisa answered.

***

That evening as Pete and Lisa got ready for supper, Lisa said, "I wish I could wear something pretty for you, instead of this plain Amish dress."

"Oh, I've been thinking all week that you look pretty in that dress."

"What, really?" she asked.

"Yes, I'm serious. I like it when you wear your hair up like that, too. It makes me think of how you looked in high school when you always wore your hair in a ponytail."

"What, you liked that?" Lisa looked at Pete with a big smile and raised her eyebrows.

"Yes, I liked that. Why do you think I asked you out on a date?"

"I don't know," Lisa said with sparkling eyes. "I just thought you were overlooking my silly ways. I've been trying to straighten my hair and get a tan so that you would find me more attractive."

"I've always thought of you as attractive," he whispered, and she watched his mouth. "I just think you look even prettier with your hair up and without makeup."

After supper, Dory said, "Let's all go out and sit on the porch for a while."

"Go tell Grandpa and Grandma to come join us," Cephas told his little daughters.

Natalie, Ida, and Orpha raced off the porch and ran over to Jonas' grandpa house. Lisa and Dory sat together on the porch swing, and Lisa held baby Toby, dawdling him on her knees. Cephas and James brought out extra chairs for the adults to sit on. The teenagers sat on the porch steps, and Natalie and the little children lay on their stomachs while coloring in coloring books. Jonas and Mattie came over and sat on a set of rocking chairs in the middle of it all. They enjoyed visiting and eating popcorn together.

"I've always been a person that believed in progress and thought that modern inventions made life better," Pete told them all. "After a week on this farm, I must admit, modern inventions haven't improved anything. In fact, I think we lost a lot."

"Let's sing a hymn," Dory said. The Amish family began singing *Amazing Grace*, and Pete's family joined in.

Church

Birds were singing lovely songs as both families gathered in front of the white farmhouse. Two double-buggies were waiting with tall, dark horses hitched to them. Cephas spoke to Pete, "You know how to drive horses now. You and your family can follow us. I'll go slow; you can let Todd follow us close. He's an older horse, and he'll follow our buggy unless you try to make him go another way."

"Okay," Pete answered nervously.

"You'll be fine!" Cephas said with a smile."

Their families piled into the buggies. Cephas' two youngest daughters, Ida and Orpha, wanted to ride with Natalie. Carrie wanted to ride with Ada and Edna, her new best friends.

The buggies rolled smoothly over flat, paved roads between growing fields of corn, soybeans, oats, and hay. Every so often, they passed a stream peacefully flowing along beside them. Todd trotted with a nice clip-clopping sound which matched the horses on Cephas' buggy. They passed other Amish farms, where large families were climbing into buggies. They all stopped and waved at the passing families. Suddenly, Cephas' buggy turned into a farm lane, and Todd followed. They came to a stop in a circle drive. A very large group of Amish women stood near a long pole building, looking as though they were trying to figure out who the new family was. Dory appeared with her baby in arms.

"Lisa, you and the girls should get out here. The men will take care of the horses," Dory said.

Lisa looked at her husband with wide eyes, as if to say, "*Okay, here we go.*"

James jumped out of Cephas' buggy and led Todd to an empty spot in the drive. The men worked together to unhitch their horses. They tied them onto a long rope stretched tightly between a building and a grain bin. Cephas looked at Pete and told him quietly, "Just follow my lead. I will try to keep you informed about what is going on."

"Okay thanks," Pete answered with a nod and followed his friend.

As they approached the barn, they saw a large circle of men opposite the cluster of women. Cephas walked to the first man in the circle and shook his hand, then onto the next. The first man in line reached out his hand, shook Pete's tightly, gave him a friendly look, and said "Good morning." From that moment on, Pete felt perfectly welcome. He followed Cephas around the whole circle of men shaking each hand and looking each man in the eyes. As he took hold of one older man's hand, he got an extra warm smile and realized it was Jonas.

Pete and Cephas joined the circle at the end of the line and visited quietly with a man nearest them while others arrived and passed handshakes along the circle. Cephas spoke softly to the men beside him.

"This is my good friend, Pete, from Chicago." One of the men spoke to Pete in Dutch. Cephas explained, "My friend only speaks English." The other men smiled politely and visited with him in hushed English, asking questions until the next man came by to shake hands.

A few of the oldest men began to head to the doorway of the shop where services were being held. Jonas joined the other elders. Pete smiled to himself, so pleased he had the honor of knowing such a fine man. As the middle-aged men began to file inside, Cephas nudged Pete, and they took their place in line.

The inside of the shop was immaculately clean, and wooden benches without backs sat in neat rows. Pete and Cephas sat side-by-side in the middle of a large group of Amish men. Women and girls sat together in neat rows on the other side of the room. Teenage boys sat in front of the men and teenage girls toward the front on the other side. Toddlers sat near their parents, and infants were cradled in their mother's arms. At the very front of the room on the women's side, a few of the younger girls sat facing the women, possibly to save space by having a bench against the front wall. Natalie sat at the very corner, and Pete was pleased he could see his daughter's smiling face. On the men's side, a row of older men sat facing the congregation. Old Jonas sat with those men.

When everyone was finally seated, a man near Pete spoke out a clear set of numbers. Everyone picked up a songbook from the bench and found the right page. The man who chose the song began to sing a long, slow series of notes, and the others joined him. Cephas helped his visitor find the right page and line. Pete struggled to follow along with German words, but the songs were sung so slowly he could take his time figuring out which word they were on. Each word was sung with so many notes, there was plenty of time to meditate on what that word might mean. After three or four songs and a great deal of time had passed, Jonas stood up in the front and began to speak in Pennsylvania Dutch. Pete looked at Cephas and raised his eyebrows. Cephas leaned over and whispered, "Jonas is our bishop."

Jonas' words were warm and heartfelt. Even though Pete couldn't understand most of them, he found himself being moved to tears as he listened. Pete watched the other older men listening intently to Jonas preach. He also noticed the young girls, in a row facing the crowd, listening just as intently. The nearest little girl to Jonas seemed to be around ten. Pete couldn't help staring at her angelic face as she watched Jonas preach. He was so impressed that such a young girl would focus so intently, yet he also knew Jonas was a great storyteller, and his words were full of wisdom and love.

A few English words found their way into his sermon as well as some Dutch phrases which were very similar to English. At one point, Pete perceived that Jonas was telling part of what had happened at his home during the past week. Jonas' voice began to tremble, and he took out a hanky and blew his nose. Others in the room wiped their eyes, including Pete and Cephas. Lisa and Dory were sitting together among the women, also sniffling.

Jonas began to speak in English. "We have some guests with us, today. I want to say this next part in English, so they know what I'm saying. When the Heller family first came to our home, they thought they were at Amish Park." Everyone in the room chuckled, including Pete and Lisa. Jonas continued. "At first, we thought that they came to our place through some kind of mix-up or misunderstanding. As the week went on, we became sure that it was no accident. We have both learned so much from each other. We have become sure that God sent them to our home and blessed us with very dear friends."

As soon as church ended, tables were set up, and food was brought in and placed neatly on them. Everyone ate together and visited quietly with those around them. One Amish man about Pete's age looked at him and said, "You should be happy you ended up at Jonas' farm instead of Amish Park."

"I am, but why do you say that?"

"Amish Park is not very — how should I say this in English — not true to real Amish life. I've heard that the guests stay in a modern hotel that looks a little like an Amish house. The park has a couple of goats and one team of horses that they give a few hayrides with, but people don't get to have real farm experiences. Staying with Jonas and Cephas, you saw what Amish life is truly like. And, maybe you noticed this, but Jonas is such a kind man, with a lot of wisdom."

"I did see that," Pete said. "I can't even begin to say how much he helped our family."

After a delicious Amish meal, families began to gather and climb into their buggies. Lisa and Dory helped other women clear off the tables, while James, Stephen, and Cephas hitched up the horses. Pete stood and watched, amazed at how willingly Cephas' sons helped. Both families crowded into the two buggies and headed back through gorgeous farmlands. Pete and Lisa looked at each other and smiled.

"There is no way we could have planned a vacation like this," Lisa said.

"Natalie, thank you for praying for our family." Pete turned around, looked at the little girls, and saw his daughter's sweet brown eyes. "God answered your prayers." Natalie, Ida, and Orpha all smiled and nodded.

Pete and Cephas dropped their wives and children off at the house. They drove their horses behind the big barn toward the buggy shed. Cephas unhitched his team, while Pete unhooked his single horse. They led the horses inside and set about taking the harnesses off.

"I had no idea your dad was a minister," Pete said.

"He has been for years. You'd think I'd learn to be more like him, living right here on the farm with him. I guess I'm too stubborn; I have to learn things the hard way."

"Me too," Pete agreed.

They curried all three horses without having much of a conversation. Finally, Cephas spoke. "I just want to tell you that I'm sorry about judging you like I did. You worked a lot harder than I would have if I thought I was paying for a vacation." They both laughed.

"I don't know; you're a hard worker. I think you would have done more than I did," Pete told Cephas.

"I feel like I missed the chance to get to know you better this week," Cephas said.

"What do you mean?"

"Well, if I hadn't been judging you and frustrated with you, we would have had more conversations and got to know each other better."

"I'm every bit as guilty as you, and maybe more," Pete said. They gave each other an awkward hug and headed to Cephas' house. Lisa and Dory were rocking slowly on a porch swing, sitting side by side. As the men came up, Dory spoke. "We'd love to have you stay for supper."

"It's really nice of you to offer, but Lisa and I have to start back to work tomorrow. We need to get going."

Cephas helped load everything in Pete's Escalade. "This is sure a nice vehicle you have here," Cephas said while handing Pete luggage.

"Thanks, but I have to admit, I'm going to miss quiet buggy rides and driving horses."

"Good," Cephas said sharply. "Then, you'll come back for more of it sometime."

"We would love to. It would be nice if your family could come and visit us in Chicago sometime. We could take you to see some sights."

"We may just do that," Cephas said. He looked Pete in the eyes as if to prove his sincerity.

"Come on let's go!" Pete called to his daughters. Dory and Lisa gave each other a hug, and the girls told everyone goodbye.

"I'm sorry that we have to leave," Pete said to Natalie.

"It's okay. I'm ready to go home," Natalie answered.

"Really?" Lisa asked.

"Yeah, I don't like it that their bathroom doesn't have a light switch," Natalie said with a serious face. Everyone laughed. As soon as the Heller family climbed into their Escalade, Pete started up his vehicle and quickly headed out of the lane. He could see the Amish family waving to them in his rearview mirror. Nobody said anything for a while. They each looked out their windows and stared at the beautiful Amish farms. Suddenly, Carrie shouted, "Dad, I left my phone on the upstairs window ledge!"

Pete pulled into a drive to turn around. It was the same farm lane they had pulled into when they came into the area a week ago. The Amish family, which had seemed so foreign to them, looked pleasant and natural. They waved at the city people, and everyone in the SUV waved back this time. As they returned to Jonas' farm, Pete said, "Carrie, it's my fault you left your cell phone there."

"How could that be your fault?" Lisa asked.

"I rushed us out of there because I was afraid I might start crying when we left." Lisa watched her husband's face closely while he talked, obviously surprised at his words. He added, "They are the nicest people I've ever met in my life."

He wiped the corner of his eye. Lisa reached over and squeezed his hand, which lay on the armrest.

Carrie spoke up from the back. "Don't worry Dad; we'll be related to them someday."

"What do you mean?" Lisa asked.

Carrie giggled and said, "I told James that I want to marry him."

"What did James say?" Natalie questioned her sister.

"He didn't say anything, but he sure did smile."

To learn more about Thomas Nye and his
books, visit: https://amishhorses.blogspot.
com/

Made in the
USA
Lexington, KY